For my nieces and nephews - Tyler, Madisyn, Sabrina, Jake, and Brad. I wish them health, happiness, and a positive mental attitude. These lessons can be applied no matter your age.

Love,
Uncle Brian

www.mascotbooks.com

The Magic Zoo

For more information, please contact:
Mascot Books
560 Herndon Parkway #120
Herndon, VA 20170
info@mascotbooks.com

CPSIA Code: PRT0915A
ISBN-13: 978-1-63177-052-4

Printed in the United States

Brian Gryn

illustrated by **Jason Buhajiar**

Gary the Guide exclaimed, "Welcome to the Magic Zoo! This zoo will change you forever!"

They looked at each other, smiling. Sabrina asked, "Where to first?"

Gary the Guide suggested, "Let's start the tour with the King of the Jungle - the lion!"

Madisyn asked, "How did he become the King of the Jungle?"

To the children's surprise, Larry the Lion walked up to them and said, "It's my positive mental attitude whenever something hasn't gone my way that has helped me become #1 in the jungle!"

"Staying positive when I get frustrated with my math homework would really help me get an A," Tyler admitted.

"That's correct, Tyler," said Larry. "Staying positive will help get you through almost any situation."

After arriving at the monkey pen, Sabrina turned to the other children and said, "These are my favorite animals. They're so playful and so good at jumping!"

"I am great at jumping because I never use the word 'can't' and I always tell myself 'I can do it, I can do it' over and over," said Mike the Monkey.

"Wow," Tyler said. "I am never saying 'can't' ever again!"

"That's right, kids. In order to become great at anything, we have to eliminate the word 'can't'," explained Gary the Guide.

Next to the monkey pen, there were two pigs rolling in the mud. Both the pigs noticed that Tyler was eating his popcorn too fast.

Peter the Pig spoke up and said, "You should eat slowly and make sure you chew your food or else you will get a tummy ache."

Tyler immediately slowed down his eating. After visiting the pigs, the kids visited a mother and baby kangaroo.

Madisyn was licking her ice cream cone and it slipped out of her hand. Sabrina laughed and said, "That's too bad. My ice cream is delicious!"

The mother kangaroo, Carol, hopped over and said to Sabrina, "Treat people like you would want to be treated." Sabrina agreed and apologized to her sister.

Madisyn was crying and very upset so Carol consoled her and said, "Whenever you get upset, make sure to take a deep breath."

Madisyn immediately took a deep breath and her crying slowed.

Jake's favorite animal was the elephant, so they went to see a big pack of elephants waiting in line to get water from a stream.

Jake commented, "Why are they all waiting? Couldn't the big ones just push the others out of the way?"

Elle the Elephant turned to Jake and explained, "Jake, having patience is really important because sometimes you are not first in line."

Gary the Guide explained, "Patience means being able to accept certain situations without getting annoyed."

Jake nodded and said, "Next time I have to wait in line for the school bus, I will wait patiently!"

Brad couldn't wait to see the tallest animal at the zoo – the giraffe! When they arrived, Brad asked, "How did you get so tall?"

Gilbert the Giraffe replied, "I eat my greens every day and you should too."

"Neat!" said Brad. "I will start eating green veggies every day so I can be big and tall!"

They moved to the next habitat and Sabrina watched the cheetahs run up and down as fast as lightning.

"Why are they running so much?" she wondered aloud.

Chris the Cheetah turned to her and said, "We run so we can be healthy and happy!"

Sabrina nodded her head. "Wow! I am going to start running during recess so I can be healthy!"

The kids ran to the big tank to watch the dolphins. It was amazing to watch them communicate in the water. Dan the Dolphin always listens to his parents by hearing the sounds bounce off the walls!

Tyler asked Dan the Dolphin, "Why do you listen so well?"

Dan responded, "I listen to my parents because I want to be a good boy and not get in trouble. That way I'm allowed to play with the rest of my dolphin friends.

After they saw the dolphins, Gary the Guide brought the kids to the shark tank.
The sharks had sharp teeth that stuck out in every direction.

Brad said, "Don't those teeth hurt your mouths? Why aren't you guys
complaining about the pain?"

Sammy the Shark explained, "We don't complain and are grateful for what we have. We get to swim all day every day. We count ourselves lucky. Some animals never get to do such a thing!"

Brad nodded his head. Most kids never get to go through The Magic Zoo and he felt super lucky and grateful!

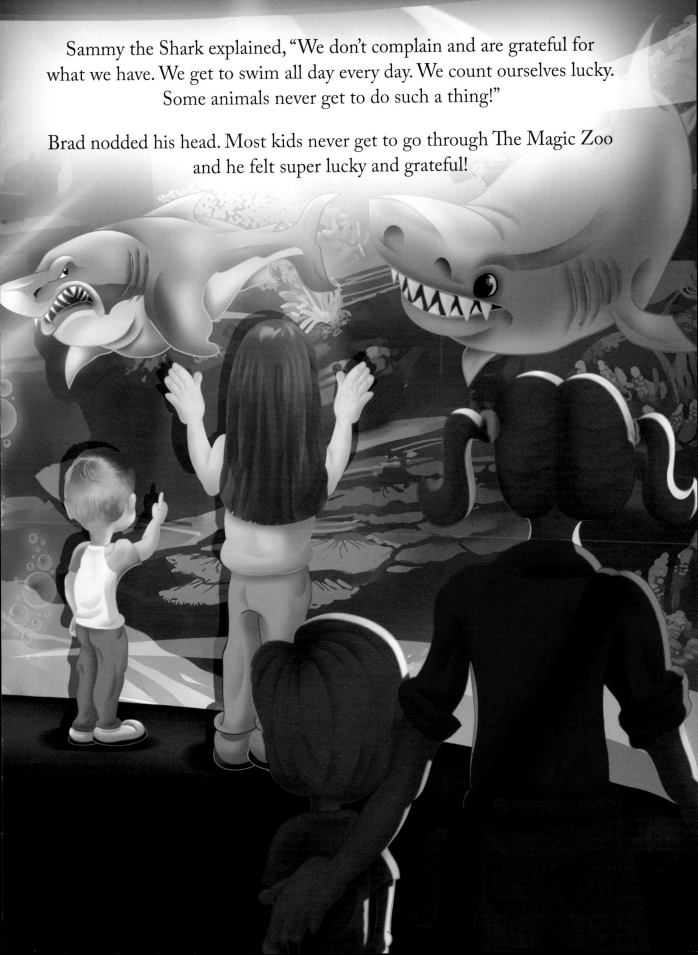

The kids were almost ready to go when they saw a group of tigers.
The children read a sign outside the habitat that said every tiger has a
unique pattern of stripes that can be used to identify it.

Timmy the Tiger strolled over and told the kids, "Be yourself. We are all different and unique which makes us each special."

The children all nodded and realized that being different, just like the tigers' stripes, was very important.

Leaving the tiger pen, the children saw a group of parrots singing so loud the whole zoo could hear them.

Philip the Parrot walked up and asked the kids, "How are you guys doing today?"

The children responded, "Good!"

Philip the Parrot quickly responded, "Kids, whenever anyone asks me how I am doing I respond, 'Excellent!' Make sure you do the same."

As they were heading to the exit, it started to get dark. The kids decided to check out the owls.

The big owl, Oliver, said, "Thanks for visiting the zoo! Be sure to think of having a great day tomorrow before you go to sleep. That's what I do before I doze off."

The children replied together, "Thanks, Oliver! We will do the same."

Gary the Guide was closing the gates to the zoo and reminded the kids, "Make sure you remember all the messages of The Magic Zoo and share them with all your friends."

The kids chorused, "We will!"

Gary reminded them, "If you have a positive mental attitude, you too can become the King of the Jungle!"

Fill in the Blank Quiz

1. Larry the Lion explained that having a _____ _____ helps you become King of the Jungle. (Hint: PMA)

2. Mike the Monkey could jump very high because he did not use the word _____.

3. Peter the Pig wants to make sure you are eating _____ in order to avoid a stomach ache. (Hint: opposite of fast)

4. Carol the Kangaroo said that the children should be nice and treat people _____.

5. Carol also urged Madisyn that whenever she gets upset she should _____.

6. Elle the Elephant told Jake that having _____ was important whenever you are waiting in line.

7. Gilbert the Giraffe explained to Brad that the best way to get big and tall was to eat _____ every day.

8. Chris the Cheetah was running up and down the grass in order to be _____.

9. Dan the Dolphin _____ to his mom and dad which allowed him to play with his dolphin friends.

10. Sammy the Shark explained that even if things aren't the way we like them, we shouldn't _____ and be _____ for what we do have.

11. Timmy the Tiger had unique stripes on his body and taught the kids to be _____ because everybody is special in their own way.

12. When you ask Phillip the Parrot, "How are you?" he responds, "I am _____."

13. Oliver the Owl mentioned that before you go to sleep at night you should think about having a _____.

About the Author

Brian Gryn was inspired by his nieces and nephews to write *The Magic Zoo*. It is never too early to learn simple life lessons like having a positive mental attitude. His goal is to spread this and many other lessons to kids in a fun way that will help inspire them to live a happy, healthy life.

Brian went to Glenbrook South H.S. in Glenview, Illinois. Brian spent two years at Butler University in Indianapolis before graduating from Indiana University's Kelley School of Business. Brian spent four years in commercial lending before becoming a personal trainer / health coach / obsessed golfer and internet entrepreneur.

Brian has two older sisters, two nieces, three nephews, and two loving parents. He currently lives in Chicago, Illinois.

For more information about the author, visit his website at briangryn.com.